GONE IS GONE

GONE IS GONE

OR

THE STORY OF A MAN WHO WANTED TO DO HOUSEWORK

RETOLD AND ILLUSTRATED
by WANDA GÁG

UNIVERSITY OF MINNESOTA PRESS
MINNEAPOLIS · LONDON

The Fesler–Lampert Minnesota Heritage Book Series

This series is published with the generous assistance of the
John K. and Elsie Lampert Fesler Fund and David R. and
Elizabeth P. Fesler. Its mission is to republish significant out-of-
print books that contribute to Minnesota's cultural legacy and to
our understanding and appreciation of the Upper Midwest.

Published by the University of Minnesota Press
111 Third Avenue South, Suite 290
Minneapolis, MN 55401-2520
http://www.upress.umn.edu

ISBN 978-0-8166-4243-4

A Cataloging-in-Publication record for this book is available
from the Library of Congress.

Printed in the United States of America on acid-free paper

The University of Minnesota is an equal-opportunity
educator and employer.

20 19 18 17 16 15 14   10 9 8 7 6 5 4 3

TO MY

PEASANT ANCESTORS

GONE IS GONE

This is an old, old story which my grandmother told me when I was a little girl. When she was a little girl her grandfather had told it to her, and when he was a little peasant boy in Bohemia, his mother had told it to him. And where she heard it, I don't know, but you can see it is an old old story, and here it is, the way my grandmother used to tell it.

It is called . . . . . .

GONE IS GONE

AND IT IS THE STORY OF A MAN
WHO WANTED TO DO HOUSEWORK

This man, his name was Fritzl—his wife, her name was Liesi. They had a little baby, Kinndli by name, and

Spitz who was a dog.

They had one cow, two goats, three pigs, and of geese they had a dozen. That's what they had.

They lived on a patch of land, and that's where they worked.

Fritzl had to plow the ground, sow the seeds and hoe the weeds. He had to cut the hay and rake it too, and stack it up in bunches in the sun. The man worked hard, you see, from day to day.

Liesi had the house to clean, the soup to cook, the butter to churn, the barn yard and the baby to care for. She, too, worked hard each day as you can plainly see.

They both worked hard, but Fritzl

always thought that he worked harder. Evenings when he came home from the field, he sat down, mopped his face with his big red handkerchief, and said: "Hu! How hot it was in the sun today, and how hard I did work. Little do you know, Liesi, what a man's work is like, little do you know! *Your* work now, 'tis nothing at all."

" 'Tis none too easy," said Liesi.

"None too easy!" cried Fritzl. "All you do is to putter and potter around the house a bit—surely there's nothing hard about such things."

"Nay, if you think so," said Liesi,

"we'll take it turn and turn about tomorrow. I will do your work, you can do mine. I will go out in the fields and cut the hay, you can stay here at home and putter and potter around. You wish to try it—yes?"

Fritzl thought he would like that well enough—to lie on the grass and

keep an eye on his Kinndli-girl, to
sit in the cool shade and churn, to
fry a bit of sausage and cook a little
soup. Ho! that would be easy! Yes,
yes, he'd try it.

Well, Liesi lost no time the next
morning. There she was at peep of

day, striding out across the fields with a jug of water in her hand and the scythe over her shoulder.

And Fritzl, where was he? He was in the kitchen, frying a string of juicy sausages for his breakfast. There he sat, holding the pan over the fire, and as the sausage was sizzling and frizzling in the pan, Fritzl was lost in pleasant thoughts.

"A mug of cider now," that's what he was thinking. "A mug of apple cider with my sausage—that would be just the thing."

No sooner thought than done.

Fritzl set the pan on the edge of the fire place, and went down into the cellar where there was a big barrel full of cider. He pulled the bung from

the barrel and watched the cider spurt
into his mug, sparkling and foaming
so that it was a joy to see.

But Hulla! What was that noise up in the kitchen—such a scuffle and clatter! Could it be that Spitz-dog after the sausages? Yes, that's what it was, and when Fritzl reached the top of the stairs, there he was, that dog, dashing out of the kitchen door with the string of juicy sausages flying after him.

Fritzl made for him, crying, "Hulla! Hulla! Hey, hi, ho, hulla!" But the

dog wouldn't stop. Fritzl ran, Spitz ran too. Fritzl ran fast, Spitz ran faster, and the end of it was that the dog got away and our Fritzl had to give up the chase.

"Na, na! What's gone is gone,"
said Fritzl, shrugging his shoulders.
And so he turned back, puffing and
panting, and mopping his face with
his big red handkerchief.

But the cider, now! Had he put the bung back in the barrel? No, that he hadn't, for here he was still holding the bung in his fist.

With big fast steps Fritzl hurried home, but it was too late, for look!

the cider had filled the mug and had run all over the cellar besides.

Fritzl looked at the cellar full of cider. Then he scratched his head and said, "Na, na! What's gone is gone."

Well, now it was high time to churn the butter. Fritzl filled the churn with good rich cream, took it under a tree and began to churn with all his might. His little Kinndli was out there too, playing Moo-cow among the daisies. The sky was blue, the sun right gay and golden, and the flowers, they were like angels' eyes blinking in the grass.

"This is pleasant now," thought Fritzl, as he churned away. "At last I can rest my weary legs. But wait! What about the cow? I've forgotten

all about her and she hasn't had a
drop of water all morning, poor thing."

With big fast steps Fritzl ran to
the barn, carrying a bucket of cool
fresh water for the cow. And high
time it was, I can tell you, for the
poor creature's tongue was hanging
out of her mouth with the long thirst

that was in her. She was hungry
too, as a man could well see by the
looks of her, so Fritzl took her from
the barn and started off with her to
the green grassy meadow.

But wait! There was that Kinndli

to think of—she would surely get into trouble if he went out to the meadow. No, better not take the cow to the meadow at all. Better keep her nearby on the roof. The roof? Yes, the roof! Fritzl's house was not covered with shingles or tin or tile— it was covered with moss and sod, and a fine crop of grass and flowers grew there.

To take the cow up on the roof was not so hard as you might think, either. Fritzl's house was built into

the side of a hill. Up the little hill,
over a little shed, and from there to
the green grassy roof. That was all
there was to do and it was soon done.

The cow liked it right well up there on the roof and was soon munching away with a will, so Fritzl hurried back to his churning.

But Hulla! Hui! What did he see there under the tree? Kinndli was climbing up on the churn—the churn was tipping!

spilling!

falling!
and now, there on the grass lay

Kinndli, all covered with half-churned cream and butter.

"So that's the end of our butter," said Fritzl, and blinked and blinked his blue eyes. Then he shrugged his shoulders and said, "Na, na! What's gone is gone."

He picked up his dripping Kinndli and set her in the sun to dry. But the sun, now! It had climbed high up into the heavens. Noontime it was, no dinner made, and Liesi would soon be home for a bite to eat.

With big fast steps Fritzl hurried off to the garden. He gathered potatoes and onions, carrots and cabbages, beets and beans, turnips, parsley and celery.

"A little of everything, that will make a good soup," said Fritzl as he went back to the house, his arms so full of vegetables that he could not even close the garden gate behind him.

He sat on a bench in the kitchen and began cutting and paring away. How the man did work, and how the peelings and parings did fly!

But now there was a great noise

above him. Fritzl jumped to his feet.

"That cow," he said, "she's sliding around right much up there on the roof. She might slip off and break her neck."

Up on the roof went Fritzl once more, this time with loops of heavy rope. Now listen carefully, and I will tell you what he did with it. He took one end of the rope and tied it around the cow's middle. The other end of the rope he dropped down the chimney and this he pulled through the fireplace in the kitchen below.

And then? And then he took the end of the rope which was hanging out of the fireplace and tied it around his own middle with a good tight knot. That's what he did.

"Oh yo! Oh ho!" he chuckled.

"That will keep the cow from falling off the roof." And he began to whistle as he went on with his work.

He heaped some sticks on the fireplace and set a big kettle of water
over it.

"Na, na!" he said. "Things are
going as they should at last, and
we'll soon have a good big soup!

Now I'll put the vegetables in the kettle—"

And that he did.

"And now I'll put in the bacon—"

And that he did too.

"And now I'll light the fire—"

But that he never did, for just then, with a bump and a thump, the cow slipped over the edge of the roof after all; and Fritzl—well, he was whisked up into the chimney and there he dangled, poor man, and couldn't get up and couldn't get down.

Before long, there came Liesi home
from the fields with the water jug
in her hand and the scythe over her
shoulder.

But Hulla! Hui! What was that

hanging over the edge of the roof? The cow? Yes, the cow, and half-choked she was, too, with her eyes bulging and her tongue hanging out.

Liesi lost no time. She took her scythe—and ritsch! rotsch!—the rope was cut, and there was the cow wobbling on her four legs, but alive and well, heaven be praised!

Now Liesi saw the garden with its gate wide open. There were the pigs and the goats and all the geese too. They were full to bursting, but the garden, alas! was empty.

Liesi walked on, and now what did she see? The churn upturned, and Kinndli there in the sun, stiff and sticky with dried cream and

butter.

Liesi hurried on. There was Spitz-
dog on the grass. He was full of
sausages and looked none too well.

Liesi looked at the cellar. There
was the cider all over the floor and
halfway up the stairs besides.

Liesi looked in the kitchen. The
floor! It was piled high with peelings
and parings, and littered with dishes
and pans.

At last Liesi saw the fireplace. Hu! Hulla! Hui! What was that in the soup-kettle? Two arms were waving, two legs were kicking, and a gurgle, bubbly and weak-like, was coming up out of the water.

"Na, na! What can this mean?" cried Liesi. She did not know (but we do—yes?) that when she saved the cow outside, something happened to Fritzl inside. Yes, yes, as soon as the cow's rope was cut, Fritzl, poor man, he dropped down the chimney and crash! splash! fell right into the kettle of soup in the fireplace.

Liesi lost no time. She pulled at the two arms and tugged at the two legs—and there, dripping and spluttering, with a cabbage-leaf in his hair,

celery in his pocket, and a sprig of
parsley over one ear, was her Fritzl.

"Na, na, my man!" said Liesi. "Is that the way you keep house—yes?"

"Oh Liesi, Liesi!" sputtered Fritzl. "You're right—that work of yours, 'tis none too easy."

" 'Tis a little hard at first," said Liesi, "but tomorrow, maybe, you'll do better."

"Nay, nay!" cried Fritzl. "What's gone is gone, and so is my housework from this day on. Please, please, my Liesi—let me go back to my work in the fields, and never more will I say that my work is harder than yours."

"Well then," said Liesi, "if that's how it is, we surely can live in peace and happiness for ever and ever."

And that they did.

THE END

GONE IS GONE

ABOUT THE BOOK

"When I was a child," says Wanda Gág, "my favorite funny Märchen was one about a peasant who wanted to do housework. I have never forgotten either the tale itself or the inimitable way in which it was told to me in German. Recently while reading Grimm's Märchen with the idea of illustrating them, I could hardly wait to come upon that old peasant fairy tale of my childhood. To my surprise and disappointment, it was not in Grimm at all. One story did slightly resemble it, but it lacked the most dramatic incident and had a different central theme. No doubt this tale exists in some German collections. There must be English versions of it too, for by questioning various children, I found them to be familiar with it, but only vaguely so. From this I concluded that it had never been presented to them as it had been to me—that is, in a full-flavored, conversational style and with a sly peasant humor which has made the tale unforgettable to me. It was for this reason that I decided to make a little book of the story, consulting no other sources except one—my own memory of how the tale was told to me when I was a little girl."